The Three Little Pigs

by Dara Goldman

Troll

Printed in China

10   9   8   7   6   5   4   3   2

Once upon a time there were three little pigs...

Pokey . . . Lazy . . .

and Will.

One sunny morning they said good-bye to their mama and papa and set off to build homes of their own.

Pokey didn't like to work hard, so he built his house out of straw.

Then he had time to play all day long.

Lazy didn't like to work hard either. He built his house out of twigs, and he had time to play all day, too.

But Will worked very, very hard. He built his house out of bricks. It took a long, long time, but the little house was solid and sturdy.

One day, not long after the pigs had built their homes, a big, bad wolf came along. He knocked on Pokey's door.

"Little pig, little pig, let me come in!" he said.

"Not by the hair on my chinny chin chin," said Pokey.

"Then I'll huff, and I'll puff, and I'll blow your house down!" said the wolf.

And he huffed, and he puffed, and he blew the
straw house down.

Pokey ran away just in time. He didn't stop running until he reached Lazy's house.

But the big, bad wolf followed Pokey.
He knocked on Lazy's door.

"Little pigs, little pigs, let me
come in!" he said.

"Not by the hairs on our chinny
chin chins," said Pokey and Lazy.

"Then I'll huff, and I'll puff,
and I'll blow your house
down!" said the wolf.

And he huffed, and he puffed, and he blew the twig house down.

Pokey and Lazy ran through the blowing
twigs and headed straight to Will's house.

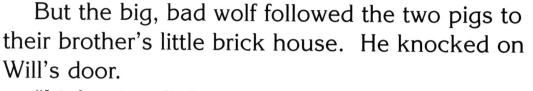

But the big, bad wolf followed the two pigs to their brother's little brick house. He knocked on Will's door.

"Little pigs, little pigs, let me come in!" he said.

"Not by the hairs on our chinny chin chins," they said.

"Then I'll huff, and I'll puff, and I'll blow your house down!" said the wolf.

And he huffed, and he puffed . . . and he puffed, and he huffed . . .

but the big, bad wolf couldn't blow the brick house down.

Then the wolf had an idea. He climbed up to
the top of the house and headed down the
chimney.
"Oh, no!" cried Pokey and Lazy.

But Will had an idea, too. The big, bad wolf fell
right in the middle of a boiling pot of soup.

"Ow! Ow! Ow!" cried the big, bad wolf. He jumped out of the pot and ran away from the little brick house as fast as he could.

And the big, bad wolf never bothered the three little pigs again.